Wizard Prince

First published in 2011
by Wayland

Text copyright © Anne Cassidy
Illustration copyright © Martin Remphry

Wayland
338 Euston Road
London NW1 3BH

Wayland Australia
Level 17/207 Kent Street
Sydney, NSW 2000

Series Editor: Louise John
Editor: Katie Powell
Cover design: Paul Cherrill
Design: D.R.ink
Consultant: Shirley Bickler

A CIP catalogue record for this book is available from the British Library.

ISBN 9780750263238

Printed in China

Wayland is a division of Hachette Children's Books,
an Hachette UK Company

www.hachette.co.uk

Wizard Prince

Written by Anne Cassidy
Illustrated by Martin Remphry

WAYLAND

Characters

Wizzle: an unfortunate wizard

Wanda: a brave girl

Prince Peter: a naughty prince

The king: an impatient king

The queen: a bossy queen

Storyteller

Storyteller: The king and queen have decided to hold a picnic in the castle gardens. Prince Peter is coming and so are Wizzle the wizard and his sister, Wanda.

Storyteller: Everyone is walking across the drawbridge into the garden. The sun is shining and the king and queen are in a very good mood!

6

King: Don't forget to bring the jelly, Wizzle. I love jelly!

 Queen: Wanda, please bring Prince Peter's toy box. He'll want to play with his toys later.

Prince Peter: I don't want to play with toys! I want to be a wizard.

 King: Wizzle, teach Prince Peter some spells.

 Prince Peter: Wait! I need a wand first. Real wizards always have wands.

 Queen: Wizzle, give Prince Peter your wand so he can be a real wizard.

Storyteller: Wizzle isn't at all happy about giving up his wand, but how can he refuse the queen?

 Wizzle: Please be careful with it, Prince Peter. I'll show you my magic spell book, too.

Wizzle: First you need to mix a spider's web with some silver glitter.

 Wanda: Don't forget the shark's tooth.

Wizzle: Now you say, 'Izzle! Wizzle! Woo!'

 **Prince Peter:** Izzle! Wizzle! Woo!

Storyteller: Just then the cauldron begins to smoke.

 Queen: Oh, look! Prince Peter is waving the wand.

King: His toy rabbit is coming to life. The spell is working. Well done, Peter!

 Storyteller: The king and queen really are very proud of Prince Peter. They clap and cheer loudly.

Storyteller: Prince Peter and Wizzle say another spell.

 Queen: Peter, you clever boy. You've made the parrot talk.

Storyteller: But Prince Peter is getting bored now. The rabbit has hopped off into the bushes and the parrot has flown away.

Storyteller: So, when no one is looking, Prince Peter picks up Wizzle's wand again. Suddenly Wanda sees what Peter is about to do!

Prince Peter: Izzle! Wizzle! Woo!

 **Wanda:** No, not your teddy!
You'll turn it into a real bear
and real bears are...

Queen: SCARY!

King: Quick, everyone. Run as fast as you can!

 Wanda: Climb that tree over there!

20

Storyteller: Everyone clambers up the tree. The bear growls at them all from the ground.

 Queen: Wizzle, I command you to get rid of that bear right now!

Storyteller: Poor Wizzle! Try as he might, nothing works!

King: You're the worst wizard in the world. The bear is eating all my jelly! You must fix this right away!

Storyteller: With that, the king, queen and Prince Peter turn their backs on Wanda and Wizzle.

Wizzle: Wanda, what can I do?

 Wanda: You have to reverse the spell! The bear has fallen asleep. Now's your chance!

 Wizzle: I can't! I have the
spider's web and the silver glitter
but I dropped the shark's tooth
when we climbed the tree.

Wanda: Look, it's over there by the bear's paw. I'll climb down and get it!

 Prince Peter: Watch out! The bear is waking up!

Storyteller: Wanda stands very still. No one makes a sound. The bear gives a loud snore as Wanda picks up the shark's tooth and throws it to Wizzle.

 Wizzle: Woo Wizzle Izzle! Woo Wizzle Izzle!

Prince Peter: Wizzle is chanting the spell backwards and the animals are turning back into toys!

 King: Well done, Wizzle! You're not such a bad wizard after all!

Storyteller: Everyone climbs down from the tree. Prince Peter bends down and picks up something from the grass.

 Prince Peter: I still want to be a wizard!

 Wanda: I think we have had quite enough magic for one day, don't you?

Prince Peter: Pizzle, Dizzle, Sizzle, Moo!

 King: Oh, no! Peter has got Wizzle's wand. Someone help me! HELP!

START READING is a series of highly enjoyable books for beginner readers. **The books have been carefully graded to match the Book Bands widely used in schools.** This enables readers to be sure they choose books that match their own reading ability.

Look out for the Band colour on the book in our Start Reading logo.

The Bands are:

Pink Band 1A & 1B

Red Band 2

Yellow Band 3

Blue Band 4

Green Band 5

Orange Band 6

Turquoise Band 7

Purple Band 8

Gold Band 9

START READING books can be read independently or shared with an adult. They promote the enjoyment of reading through satisfying stories supported by fun illustrations.

Anne Cassidy has written lots of books for children. Many of them are about talking animals who get into trouble. She has two dogs, Charlie and Dave, but, sadly, neither of them talk to her! This time she wanted to write about a funny wizard who gets his spells mixed up.

Martin Remphry grew up on the tiny Channel Island of Sark. He has always loved drawing, especially spooky things such as witches and wizards, so it was a dream come true for him to illustrate Wizzle. He loves the funny ingredients Wizzle uses for his spells, even if they don't always work as he hopes!